BeastQuest
NEW BLOOD
ADAM BLADE

ORCHARD

With special thanks to Allan Frewin Jones

For my friend, John Wilkinson

ORCHARD BOOKS

First published in Great Britain in 2019 by The Watts Publishing Group

3 5 7 9 10 8 6 4 2

Text © 2019 Beast Quest Limited
Cover illustrations by KJA Artists © Beast Quest Limited 2019
Inside illustrations by Dynamo © Beast Quest Limited 2019

Beast Quest is a registered trademark of Beast Quest Limited
Series created by Beast Quest Limited, London

A CIP catalogue record for this book is available from the British Library.

ISBN 978 1 40835 785 9

Printed in Great Britain

MIX
Paper from
responsible sources
FSC® C104740

The paper and board used in this book are made from wood from responsible sources

Orchard Books
An imprint of Hachette Children's Group
Part of The Watts Publishing Group Limited
Carmelite House, 50 Victoria Embankment, London EC4Y 0DZ

An Hachette UK Company
www.hachette.co.uk
www.hachettechildrens.co.uk

BeastQuest
NEW BLOOD
ADAM BLADE

ORCHARD

MEET THE GUARDIANS

SAM

BEAST POWER: Fire
LIKES: The beach
DISLIKES: Being told what to do

AMY

BEAST POWER: Storm
LIKES: Sports
DISLIKES: Injustice

CHARLIE

BEAST POWER: Water
LIKES: Puzzles
DISLIKES: Heights

PROLOGUE

Karita of Banquise gazed in awe at Tom, Avantia's mighty, bearded Master of the Beasts. Legendary hero and defender of the kingdom, for twenty years Tom had victoriously faced down foul creatures, powerful magical terrors and grotesque invasions from enemy realms. Among Avantia's protectors he had no equal. He was also Karita and her companions' mentor, advisor and friend.

Under his leadership, she and the others would today face their greatest challenge.

Tom pointed towards the brooding Gorgonian castle.

"We must recover the chest of Beast eggs Malvel stole," he reminded them. His fierce blue eyes moved from Karita to the others: Dell of Stonewin, whose bloodline connected him to Beasts of Fire; Fern of Errinel, linked to Storm Beasts; Gustus of Colton, bonded with Water Beasts.

"Malvel will be expecting an attack," Tom said. "His power is diminished, but he is still formidable." His eyes locked on Karita. "Stealth will be our greatest ally."

Karita felt as though her whole life

had been a preparation for this moment. Countless hours spent studying the ancient tomes, day after day of gruelling combat training, months learning how to influence the will of Stealth Beasts and control the powers that filled the Arcane Band at her wrist.

But was she ready?

She gazed into Tom's face, and her doubts faded.

Yes!

A low rumble came from the castle. Flashes of green lightning spat into the clouds as a swarm of screeching creatures erupted from the battlements.

Karita shuddered as Malvel's hideous

minions streaked through the sky toward them. They were man-sized, with dark hides, limbs tipped with hooked claws, and gaping jaws lined with sharp teeth. Their leathery wings cracked like whips.

"Karrakhs!" muttered Tom. "Karita – go!"

She nodded and slipped away behind jagged-edged rocks. She turned to see the swarm of foul creatures engulf her companions. Tom's sword flashed. Howls rang out from the Karrakhs. The Guardians were using their Arcane Bands to form weapons that spun and crushed!

Karita raced for the castle, keeping low behind the ridge of rocks. Reaching the walls, she climbed up a gnarled vine and

10

crawled through a narrow window. She looked back again to see that Tom and the Guardians had battled their way through the castle gates.

Well fought!

She dropped into a wide room filled with bookcases and crept to the door. Torches burned in the corridor, sending shadows leaping. The castle was silent, but Karita felt a growing dread as she slipped along the walls.

She knew where the chest of Beast eggs was hidden.

But how fiercely would it be guarded?

She came to a circular room, and saw the chest standing against the wall. She was surprised not to see any of Malvel's forces in sight. *Strange ...* As she approached the chest, she checked the walls and floor for traps and other hidden dangers. Her heart hammering, Karita opened the lid and gazed down at the eggs. They were different sizes, shapes and colours. One slipped from the pile and she caught it in her gloved hand. It was pale blue, about the size of a goose egg. Acting on instinct, she slipped it inside her breastplate.

CRASH!

She spun around. Malvel stood against the room's closed door, his eyes burning.

"Did you really think you could enter my domain unseen?" he snarled, a green glow igniting in his palm. His voice was weaker than she'd imagined. "I *wanted* you to come here. After all, only a Guardian can hatch a Beast egg."

Karita swallowed hard, seeking a way to escape.

"You and your friends will hatch these Beasts and I will drink in their power," growled the wizard. "I will become mighty again and Avantia will bow before me!"

"I'm not afraid of you!" Karita shouted.

A ball of green fire exploded from Malvel's hand. Karita dived aside, seared by the heat.

She leaped up, thrusting her right arm towards the wizard. Her Arcane Band began to form a weapon, but another blast of fire sent her sliding across the floor.

Malvel loomed over her, both hands burning green. Before he could strike, the door burst open and Tom and the other Guardians rushed into the room.

"No!" roared Malvel. "Where are my Karrakhs?"

"Defeated!" shouted Tom, whirling his sword to deflect Malvel's green flames. "Guardians! Take the eggs!"

Fern dived for the chest, but a blast from the wizard knocked her off her feet.

"The eggs are mine!" howled Malvel. He traced a large circle of fire in the air. There was a blast of hot wind as the flaming hoop crackled and spat.

Malvel snatched up the chest and turned to the black heart of the fiery circle.

"He's opened a portal!" shouted Tom. "Stop him!"

Gustus ran at the wizard and seized the chest from his grip. Roaring in anger, Malvel launched a fireball, but Fern managed to shove Gustus out of its path. But the force of her push knocked Gustus into the portal. With a stifled cry, he and the chest of eggs were gone.

"No!" Fern shouted, diving in after him. With a shout, Dell ran after her.

"Wait!" shouted Tom.

"It's our duty to protect the eggs!" Dell

called back as he disappeared into the swirling portal after his two friends.

Malvel sprang forwards, but Tom bounded in front of him, holding him back with his spinning blade as the wizard hurled magical fireballs at him.

Karita noticed the walls of the portal writhing and distorting. Malvel's magical fireballs were making it unstable. At any moment it might vanish!

Tom was knocked back by a torrent of green fire as the wizard turned and leaped into the shuddering portal. Karita flung herself after him.

"No! Karita!" The last thing she heard was Tom's voice. "The portal is in flux! You could be sent anywhere!"

And then there was nothing but a rushing wind and howling darkness, as she plunged into the unknown.

ONE

"Finally, I have bequests for my granddaughter, Amy Errinel-Li, and my great-nephews, Charles Dockary Colton and Samuel Stonewin."

Amy perked up as she heard the solicitor speak her name. She'd been so bored by the reading of her grandmother's will that she'd considered turning off her cochlear implant.

But now it seemed like things might get interesting.

She whispered in her cousin's ear. "I never knew your middle name was Dockary."

"It's from my Jamaican side," Charlie whispered back. "I was named after my grandfather. What does 'bequests' mean?"

"Gifts," Amy replied softly.

"Cool!"

The two cousins were surrounded by the whole sprawling Errinel-Colton-Stonewin clan. They were gathered in the grand, wood-panelled dining room of Gran's London home. The Stonewins and the Coltons weren't really blood relations, but Gran had always treated them as family.

Even Amy's cousin Sam was there, fresh from Los Angeles – playing games on his phone, which Amy thought was kind of disrespectful. Although Charlie had only met Sam twice, he'd taken an instant dislike to his American cousin. Amy was prepared to give him the benefit of the doubt, but she had to admit, Sam did seem a bit full of himself.

Amy had loved her grandmother, and she missed her terribly. But Gran Fern had lived a good life and had died peacefully at ninety-five. Three months on, Amy was able to remember her without her heart aching so much.

And now there was an inheritance!

"Would the three children step forward to receive their bequests?" the solicitor asked.

Amy and Charlie joined Sam to walk to the head of the long table. Three hoops of engraved metal lay there, one labelled for each cousin.

Amy leaned closer, fascinated by the odd markings on the thick bracelets.

"Are they valuable?" asked Sam.

"Trust him to ask that," Charlie muttered to Amy, picking his bracelet up. "They look weird, though. Why would Aunt Fern think we'd want these?"

"They're gorgeous." Amy took her bracelet and slipped it on to her right wrist. It felt perfect, as if it was always meant to be there.

Now that the official part of the gathering was over, people got up from the table

and broke into smaller groups, chatting and catching up. A sea of noise like this sometimes made it difficult for Amy to focus on a single conversation, so she switched her implants to a better programme.

When the implant reset a few seconds later, Amy proudly showed her bracelet to her parents.

"I've never seen this jewellery before," her mum confided. "Your gran must have locked them away for some reason."

"Look after it, sweetheart," said her father.

"Oh, I will!" Amy replied.

Sam's mother, Aunt Jessica, joined them. All Amy knew about Aunt Jessica and Sam was that they'd recently moved to London from LA, and that she was a high-flying lawyer with a job at Obsidian Corp – one of the biggest companies on the planet.

"You're famous, Jess," said Amy's mother, holding out her smart phone. It showed a news article with a picture of Jessica, standing beside a tall, broad-shouldered man in a dark suit.

"Mr Haynecroft is always in the news," said Aunt Jessica. "He's a brilliant CEO."

Amy didn't much like the look of the man. His hair was slicked back from a high forehead and he had a goatee beard and a moustache. He had a strong, bony face and the eyes of a man used to being obeyed. In

25

his right hand he held a silver walking stick with a carved handle.

Amy drifted off, finding Charlie with his father.

"Jewellery, huh?" Charlie said as he waggled the bracelet at Amy.

"It's the thought that counts, son," said his father.

"And Great-Aunt Fern thought I'd want a *bracelet*?"

They all laughed.

Amy and Charlie wandered from room to room, reminiscing about the big family Christmases Fern had organised here.

They ended up in her study. It was like a library, a laboratory and a museum all mashed together; full of weird, interesting stuff that Gran had collected over her long and eventful life.

"Oh, hi." Sam stood in the doorway. "Freaky place, huh? My mom says those bracelets aren't worth squat."

"It's a gift from *Gran*," Amy said, irritated. "That's all that matters."

"If you say so," said Sam, shrugging. "Hey, were you guys making that weird noise just now?"

"What weird noise?" said Charlie. "I don't know what you mean, but it wasn't us."

Sam frowned. "It was definitely coming from in here." He lifted his hand. "There it is again. Can't you hear it?"

Amy touched the controls of her hearing processors and turned them up. There was nothing. "What does it sound like?" she asked.

"Like a baby bird calling to its mother," said Sam. He circled the room, listening intently. "How come you guys can't hear it? You're getting nothing, Chas? And I thought you were supposed to have pretty good hearing with those implants, Amy?"

"I certainly do." She touched the processors behind her ears. "Another *great* thing about them is that I can switch off annoying people."

Amy had been deaf since birth, and her hearing implants had been put in when she was a baby. She was completely at ease with her deafness and also with the processors that hooked behind her ears and the coils that attached to her head – they were part of who she was.

"Fair enough," said Sam. "Sorry if I offended you." He started, looking around the room. "But you seriously can't hear that?" He walked to the wall, pressing his ear against it. "It's really loud."

"Hearing things that aren't there?" Charlie said. "That's not a good sign, Samuel."

Sam frowned at him. "I prefer Sam."

"Then stop calling me Chas ..." Charlie's voice faded. His eyes were popping. Amy turned and saw that a panel had slid open where Sam was standing.

"Awesome!" breathed Sam, stepping into a narrow, stone-lined compartment.

"Wait," called Charlie, "you can't just barge in there."

"Why not?" said Sam. "Hey, look – there's stuff carved on the wall."

Amy and Charlie rushed over to the strange alcove. Three symbols, inside carved circles, had been etched into the stone: the first was a zigzag, like lightning; the second contained a branching shape;

and the third was three horizontal wavy lines.

Amy stared at her bracelet. The main design on it was that same zigzag inside a circle. "Look at this!" She held it up for the boys to see.

"Wow!" breathed Sam, taking his bracelet out of his pocket. It had the branching lines on it.

"Uh-oh," said Charlie. "I'm pretty sure mine has those three wiggly lines." He touched the engraving. "Yow!" He jumped back as the lines on the wall began to glow. "What *was* that? I think we should get my dad, he'll know what to—"

"No way, this is great! Just like a video

game." Sam touched his symbol and it immediately lit up from within. "Now you, Amy ..."

Full of curiosity, Amy reached out. As her symbol too began to gleam, the wall slid aside, revealing a long, dark stairway ...

TWO

Sam took out his phone and activated the torch, shining it down the stairwell. "A secret passage! Can you believe it? How cool was Fern?"

"We have to tell people about this," insisted Charlie.

"Yeah, *right*!" Sam bounded down the stairs, reaching a strange cellar that branched off in all directions. Stone pillars held up a low, vaulted brick roof.

"What's down there?" he heard Amy call, her voice echoing in the gloom.

"Come and find out." Sam didn't understand why his cousins weren't as excited as he was. Glowing symbols, a secret passage ... this was *awesome*!

Sam could hear that chirping noise again, but much louder. It was coming from a nook over to the left. He headed towards it, his phone lighting up cobwebs and old stone walls.

"It smells really dank down here," Amy said. "Sam, don't go rushing off!"

"Oh, what's the worst that can happen?" Sam said, just at the moment he felt something shift under his foot. He heard a loud scraping noise.

Behind them, the stone steps were sliding back into the wall.

"Look what you did!" yelled Charlie.

The wall leading to the high entrance was smooth. The stairway was gone.

"What did you do?" demanded Amy.

"I don't know," said Sam. "I only—" He lifted his foot and felt another movement in the ground. With a rush and a clang, a spiked iron fence shot up out of the floor, cutting Sam off from the others. "Oops."

"Stop *moving*," Amy yelled.

Sam heard a low growl behind him. He turned slowly, his heart drumming. From deep shadows, a pair of glowing red eyes stared at him. He aimed his torch beam, feeling his stomach do a backflip.

"That's not good," he muttered.

An enormous shape lurched forwards. The thing was huge and grey, its flesh crisscrossed with fiery cracks that gave off white steam. It was as if a stone gargoyle filled with lava had come alive! It had the face of a bat, with flaring nostrils and a snarling mouth that bristled with vicious-looking teeth. The monster spread its stone wings and growled, giving off a smell like rotting eggs.

What is this thing? Sam was caught somewhere between feeling scared, fascinated and repulsed.

The figure stomped towards Sam, and he bounded back, wincing at the stench. "No offence, dude, but your breath stinks. Hey, watch it!" His brain whirled as the creature's clawed hands reached for him.

"Don't let it grab you!" shrieked Amy.

"Thanks – great advice!" As the monster snatched at him with vicious stone claws, Sam ducked under its arm and dived, putting distance between them.

He's big, but slow – maybe I can outrun him?

The creature snarled and slavered as it stamped towards Sam. One swipe of those claws and he'd be dead!

He slipped behind a pillar, hearing claws scraping stone, the monster bellowing in frustration. Sam ran behind another pillar, then peeked out to see the thing lumbering closer.

This might just work!

As he darted from pillar to pillar, Sam heard Amy and Charlie yelling encouragement – but he still needed a better plan than playing hide-and-seek!

The monster let out a roar.

"I can keep this up all day!" Sam called, trying to sound more confident than he felt.

The monster rose to its full height, opening its mouth and breathing red fire

on to its clawed hands.

Uh-oh!

Sam dived aside as two whips of fire burst from the creature's fists, snaking out towards him. But he wasn't quick enough. A coil of flame wrapped around his arm, the pain searing through his body as he was dragged to his knees. He let out a scream of agony.

"Ha-*hai*!" A piercing yell echoed through the cellar and Sam gasped in relief as the blazing whip recoiled. Amy had climbed the barrier and given the monster a roundhouse kick to the belly that sent it reeling.

"Touch him again and I'll make a rockery

out of you!" she shouted, her face ferocious.

"You tell him, Amy!" called Charlie, also climbing the iron barrier.

Roaring, the monster turned on Amy, its fiery whips sizzling the air. Jerking back to avoid the flames, Amy fell. The creature loomed over her.

"No!" Sam cried, ignoring the pain in his arm as he ran forwards.

Amy lifted her hand defensively. Her bracelet flashed silver and began to flow up her arm to form a plate of gleaming metal.

A shield! Sam realised. *Awesome!*

The fire whips bounced off the shield and the monster staggered back, squealing in alarm.

Sam pulled his own bracelet out of his pocket. Could he make a shield as well?

He slipped the band over his wrist. The metal began to spread and transform. But it didn't form a shield. It turned into a long metal grappling hook on a chain.

Now we can have a real fight!

He swung the hook. It bounced off the creature's thick hide with a clang. The monster turned, twirling its fiery whips.

Charlie was on this side of the barrier now.

Amy stood up. Sam was stunned to see that her shield had somehow transformed into a silver mace. She approached the monster with a determined face.

"Charlie!" she called over her shoulder. "Use your bracelet!"

"I can't," Charlie called. "I left it with my dad!"

Great thinking, Charlie! Sam thought.

He swung his hook again, but it glanced off the monster's shoulder.

"Grab it with the hook, then Amy can pound it!" Charlie shouted.

"What do you think I'm *trying* to do?" yelled Sam as Amy darted to and fro, avoiding the whips, lunging at the monster.

Wow, she's good!

Charlie grabbed a stone off the floor and lobbed it at the creature's head ... but missed, and almost brained Sam.

43

At least he's trying, I suppose!

The monster almost had Amy cornered.

Sam tried one last desperate attack. He spun around, swinging the hook like a hammer thrower in a field event. The throw went wide, the hook hitting the ceiling and lodging among its ancient, buckling bricks.

Sam yanked at the chain with all his might. The hook came loose, sending a whole lot of masonry down on the gargoyle's back, crushing it to the floor.

Amy ducked away to protect her implants from the debris, then she leaped forwards, taking her mace in both hands and bringing it down hard where the creature's head met its body. The fire whips vanished as it crumbled away into burning coals. A low rumble sounded as the iron barrier dropped into the ground and the stairway emerged again from the wall.

"Wicked skills, Amy!" gasped Charlie. "You totally killed it!"

Amy drew her arm across her forehead. "I am *loving* this bracelet!" she said with a grin. As she lowered the mace it melted back into the wristband.

Now that the monster was gone, a sudden desperate urgency filled Sam's mind. That sound that had led him to Aunt Fern's study was calling again, filling his head with an insistent muttering.

His grappling hook melted into his bracelet as he turned and raced into the darkness.

"What on earth was that *thing*?" Charlie asked. "And what happened with your bracelets? And, Sam? Where are you going?"

"I don't know!" Sam called back.

His phone light shone on a very large egg, lying on a flat shard of stone.

Sam dropped to his knees. The egg was black with red spirals.

"*You're* making that noise," he breathed, lifting the egg in both hands. "What are you?"

He could feel a throbbing in his palms –

like a heartbeat.

As he stared in amazement, he heard a *snap* and the egg broke open in his hands.

THREE

"Oh no, what now?" Charlie asked as he and Amy found Sam kneeling on the ground with his back to them.

Sam turned to show them a small black dragon sitting on his palms, its folded wings as shiny as metal, its eyes huge and bright. It opened its muzzle and a breath of smoke floated from between its jaws.

"She hatched," said Sam, nodding towards the broken pieces of shell on the ground. "I think I'll call her Spark."

Charlie gazed at the creature in disbelief. "How do you know it's a 'her'?" he asked.

Amy stared at him. "Sam's holding a newborn dragon and *that's* all you're wondering about?"

"Isn't she lovely?" Sam said, getting to his feet while the dragon gazed adoringly up into his face. "She was calling to me from her egg. That was the sound I was hearing. How awesome is that?"

"Pretty awesome," agreed Amy. "But this is turning into a very strange day." She looked at Sam's arm. "You'll need something for the burns where that whip caught you."

"What burns?" Sam asked, resting Spark on his shoulder and rolling up the tatters of his sleeve.

Charlie gazed at Sam's arm. Although the cloth was badly scorched, his skin was clear. "How'd you not get fried?" he asked.

Sam shrugged. "No clue."

"Hey, what's that?" Amy stooped and picked something up from the slab of stone where the egg had sat. She held it up on a fine metal chain. It was an amulet with a red stone set in the middle. It looked very old.

"Fern really had a thing for jewellery," said Charlie.

"There's writing on it," Amy said, looking

closer. She began to read:

"*Children of Avantia, protect the eggs from the Dark Wizard.*" Charlie felt the hairs on the back of his neck standing up as Amy spoke. "*This is our secret and our duty. Everything depends on you.*"

"Cool!" said Sam, stroking Spark's folded wings.

"Cool?" demanded Charlie. "How is any of this cool? This isn't one of your video games. Fire monsters! A dark wizard! More freaky jewellery." He pointed to the amulet.

"Fine, if you don't like it," said Amy. "But I'm keeping it." She tucked the amulet into her shirt. "I don't know what you want us to do with this stuff, Gran," she said softly. "But I promise we won't let you down."

Charlie felt like his brain had been put in a blender. There had to be a sensible explanation for all of this, but he could think about that later. "Can we just get out of here?" he asked the others.

They headed for the stairs.

Sam helped the baby dragon perch on his shoulder. She sat there happily, giving off thin puffs of smoke. "Come on, Spark," he said, climbing the stairs. "I'll look after you."

Charlie rolled his eyes as he followed. "My dad will be able to figure all this out."

Sam turned on the stairs. "We can't tell anyone about this," he said firmly.

"You're not serious?" Charlie gasped.

"Sam's right," Amy agreed. "This started when we were given Gran's bracelets." Her eyes shone. "They were a secret, and Gran left them to *us*. Not to our parents or anyone else. She left them to *us*."

Sam nodded. "We were *meant* to find Spark." He looked at Charlie. "Come on, Chas – I mean, *Charlie* – you know we're right."

Charlie hesitated. If Amy thought they should keep quiet, maybe he could go along with them ... at least, for the moment.

"Fine," he said, pointing to Sam's hood.

"But how are you going to keep that thing secret?"

"She's not a *thing*. But I'll put her in my hood, so no one sees her." Sam grinned. "My mom has to go straight to work from here. I brought my bike so I could cycle back to the apartment. No problem."

Amy frowned. "Listen, Charlie and I have our bikes here, too. We'll go with you. Between the three of us, we should be able to come up with a good hiding place."

"And you should put her in your bag, not your hood," suggested Charlie.

"Great idea," said Sam. "OK – let's say our goodbyes and get out of here. I want to find out if Spark can fly!"

"Or breathe fire," added Amy.

That's all we need, thought Charlie. *Our own fire-breathing, flying dragon!*

FOUR

The three cousins cycled through Battersea Park on their way to the luxury Thames-side block where Sam lived.

"There's smoke coming out of your backpack again," Charlie pointed out. "That dragon is a fire hazard!"

"Spark, quit smoking back there," Sam said with a laugh.

The wisps of smoke vanished.

"Wow," gasped Amy. "She must have heard you."

"We understand one another," said Sam.

"Is he for real?" Charlie muttered to Amy.

"I heard that!" Sam exclaimed in annoyance.

They were cycling past the boating lake when a woman stepped out of the trees. She appeared so suddenly that Sam had to slam on the brakes to avoid hitting her.

"Hey, watch it, lady!" he gasped, screeching to a halt.

He goggled at her. She was the tallest woman he'd ever seen. She had long, purple-streaked black hair, and a fierce, proud face with stunningly bright green eyes. She wore a calf-length leather coat and leather boots, and carried a long whitewood pole.

"Where is the Beast?" the woman demanded, her eyes glittering like emeralds. "I sensed the hatching – I know you have it!"

"She's not a beast!" Sam retorted. *Rats ... wrong thing to say!* "Erm, I mean, I don't know what you're talking about, lady."

"Don't waste my time," demanded the woman.

"Who *are* you?" asked Amy.

The woman spun the pole in her hands. "Hand the Beast over ... or must I take it from you?"

"We've got bikes," Charlie said in a low voice. "We can get past her easily."

"I'm not so sure," Amy said. "That thing she's holding is a bo-staff. And she looks like she knows how to use it."

A bo-staff? thought Sam. *That's a martial arts weapon.* He glanced around, but the park was otherwise deserted. *This could get tricky!*

He shook himself, determined. "I'm not giving Spark to you, lady, so just back off and let us past," Sam declared. He could feel the little dragon moving about in his backpack.

The woman took on a fighting pose, aiming her bo-staff at Sam.

"What if she's the Dark Wizard the amulet warned us about?" asked Charlie. Before anyone could respond, Amy let out a yell.

"Sam! Your backpack's on fire!"

Sam twisted his head. A stream of smoke rose from his bag. A moment later, Spark burst up through a scorched hole and crawled on to his shoulder, staring at the woman and hissing fiercely.

"Oh ..." said the woman, sounding disappointed. "It's only a dragon."

"*Only*?" said Amy.

"I'll take it anyway," said the woman. "I may find a use for it."

"Not gonna happen!" shouted Sam. He

kicked hard on his pedals, leaning in as he rode straight for the woman. She'd have to jump aside, then he'd be free and clear.

In the blink of an eye, the woman was gone.

Where did she—

She appeared again at his side and jammed the bo-staff between the spokes of his front wheel. The bike came to a juddering halt and Sam went flying over the handlebars.

Years of stunting on his skateboard gave him the instinct to duck and roll as he landed, getting back to his feet as Spark flapped away, shrieking wildly.

"See what she just did!" yelled Charlie.

"I told you, she's the Dark Wizard!"

"You just messed with the wrong kids!" shouted Sam. He stretched out his right arm as his bracelet began to morph into the long hook and chain. He saw Amy drop her bike – she already had the silver mace in her fist.

Sam swung the chain around his head and launched it at the woman. She batted it aside and used the staff to vault over his head, her long coat-tails flying. Before he could turn, he felt the bo-staff hit between his shoulder blades.

"Ooofff!" He dropped to his knees, the breath driven out of him.

"I see you have Arcane Bands," said the

woman coldly. "They won't help you."

"That's what you think!" shouted Amy, running at the woman.

The woman spread her feet, thrusting with the bo-staff to parry Amy's mace, spinning around and striking Amy on the back as she stumbled past.

Sam got to his feet, winded but ready to fight. He saw Charlie trip over his bike as he tried to dismount. Charlie and the bike collapsed in a tangle.

For a moment, the woman's back was to Sam. He snatched up his fallen hook and bounded forwards. He would never use that hook on her – but if he could pin her arms with the chain, maybe Amy would be

able to batter her way through the bo-staff.
Then the three of them could make a run
for it.

He leaped at the woman – but again, she
vanished!

She reappeared close to where Charlie
was trying to untangle himself from his
bike. Amy rushed at the woman, her mace
in both hands. Moving almost faster than
Sam could take in, the woman gave Amy
three swift blows with her staff – head,
torso and arm. Amy fell sideways with
a cry, her hands grappling to protect her
implants.

Sam saw that the blows had been light –
enough to stop Amy, without really hurting

her or her implants.

"Leave her alone!" Charlie shouted as Amy struggled to get to her feet.

"Or *what*?" demanded the woman. "Children of Avantia?" she scoffed. "I think not!"

Charlie gave a yelp of surprise as his bracelet flashed silver and grew into a hefty battle-axe. "Or *this*!" he shouted, running at the woman, the axe lifted above his head.

"Impressive!" she said, vanishing and reappearing behind him. "But futile!" She swung the bo-staff low, sweeping Charlie's legs from under him.

The woman turned to Sam, the staff

between her hands, her eyes gleaming. "Let's put an end to this foolery," she said. "Give me the dragon!"

Sam heard Spark hissing. The little dragon had scurried away under cover of a bush. Plumes of thick black smoke showed where she was lurking.

I have to protect her!

Sam spun the hook above his head. "One more step and you get this!" he warned.

A sudden gush of black smoke rolled across the pathway.

Wow! So much smoke from such a little dragon!

Sam released the chain, sending the hook flying. He had intended it only to block the woman, but in the split second before he released his weapon, she vanished and reappeared right in its path. Hammering the butt of her staff into the ground, she cartwheeled out of the way – but the hook caught in her coat, ripping through it.

Within seconds, she was engulfed in the ball of thick smoke. Sam heard a crash as though she had landed badly. He could hear her coughing.

He reeled in the chain and found a piece of the woman's coat snagged on the hook. He pulled it off and stuffed it into his backpack as the weapon dissolved back into his wristband. A moment later, there was a fluttering of wings and Spark landed on his shoulder.

"Clever girl," Sam crooned. "You learned how to fly!"

With Spark safe on his shoulder, Sam ran for Amy and yanked her to her feet.

Charlie was already up, rubbing the back of his head.

The ball of dense smoke expanded rapidly, flooding out over the pathway and across the grass. Sam had never seen anything like it before.

"Come on," said Sam. "Let's get out of here."

Grabbing their bikes, they mounted and rode at breakneck speed across the grass, keeping just ahead of the spreading wall of smoke.

Sam heard the woman shouting behind them.

Yell all you like, lady! We're out of here!

Then he heard a growl from much closer by.

"What was that?" Charlie panted, struggling to keep up.

Sam glanced to one side. A pair of violet eyes stared at him through the smoke. Eyes as big as tennis balls. Huge, slitted cat's eyes.

"I don't know what it is," yelled Sam, putting on a spurt. "And I don't want to know!"

He was in the lead, but Amy and Charlie were right behind as they sped across the grass, pedalling for their lives!

FIVE

"**N**ow, what a view!" Charlie and Amy stood on the thirteenth-floor terrace of Sam's Skylight Quay flat, gazing out at the London skyline.

"Spark's making herself a nest on top of my closet," Sam said, joining them. "I think she's going to be happy here."

Amy pointed eastwards towards the cluster of skyscrapers in the area known as the City, the financial heart of London. The black finger of Obsidian Tower dominated the skyline, head and shoulders above all the other buildings. "Is that where your mum works?"

"Yeah. Mom says Obsidian Tower is really high-tech. It'd be cool to see it someday, but the security's so strict, I can't even visit her." Sam nodded. "But at least this apartment comes with the job."

"Amazing!" breathed Charlie.

A timer went off in the kitchen. "Pizza's ready!" said Sam.

Sam had put the pizza in the oven when they'd first got here. Then he'd given them a guided tour of the stunning penthouse.

They trooped inside to the kitchen. Amy

and Charlie sat at a table opposite huge windows. Everywhere you went in this flat, you could see right across London. Charlie had trouble not feeling envious.

Amy looked at her cousins. "We need to talk about what's happening. First the secret cellar, then that monster gargoyle, and now that weirdo woman."

"Don't forget the *dragon*," Charlie said. "And the bracelets that turn into *weapons*."

Sam took out the pizza and slid it on to a big plate in the middle of the table.

"Uh, Sam," Amy began, "you're not wearing oven gloves."

"Oh ... I forgot," Sam replied.

Charlie looked at Sam's hands. He had

just taken a freshly cooked pizza from the oven, and he had not been burned. He didn't even seem to notice the heat.

Sam gazed at his hands. "I'm fireproof!" he said. "How weird is that?"

"It's just one more weird thing to add to the list," said Amy. "Charlie thought that woman was the 'Dark Wizard' mentioned on the amulet," she continued. "If she is, then we—"

"I've changed my mind," Charlie said. He'd had been thinking hard about the woman. "She had the chance to pulverise us back there, and she didn't take it. I think the 'Dark Wizard' would have mashed us to a pulp."

Sam nodded. "I'm with Charlie," he said. "She was toying with us."

"I wonder what she meant when she said, *'Children of Avantia – I think not'*," Charlie mused.

"Avantia is mentioned on the amulet," said Amy.

Sam nodded. "That's right. 'Avantia' kind of sounds like it's a place. Maybe a country somewhere?"

"Maybe it's where she lives?" suggested Amy.

"Well, *I've* never heard of it," said Charlie.

"Oh! Wait up!" Sam suddenly jumped up. "I'll be back in a sec." He zipped out of the kitchen, reappearing a few moments later with a scrap of black leather in his hand.

He spread out the piece of leather on the table. "I forgot about this," he said. "It's from that lady's coat – my hook ripped it off."

"There's part of a pocket," said Amy, leaning close.

"And look here!" Sam drew out a small piece of card. "A train ticket!"

"Show me," said Charlie. He examined the ticket. "*Chillinghurst to London Terminals*," he read. "It's dated today." He narrowed his eyes. "Chillinghurst is on the Southern line out of Victoria," he said. "Trains run every hour off peak. The journey takes fifty-three minutes."

"How'd you *know* that?" breathed Sam.

"His brain is full of that sort of stuff," grinned Amy. "He's like Wikipedia on legs."

"That's amazing!" Sam said, admiringly. "Oh! And remember how that lady said she sensed Spark hatching? She sure didn't waste any time getting here!"

"We should go to Chillinghurst," said Charlie. "Maybe she lives there? That's a small town so maybe people will know her. She doesn't exactly blend in, does she?"

"True," agreed Amy. "OK – tomorrow's Saturday. How about we all meet up at Victoria Station first thing and track that weirdo woman down?"

"And start getting answers to what's going on," said Charlie, tucking into his slice of pizza. "Because I'm telling you, guys – we need to get to the bottom of this before that Dark Wizard shows up!"

SIX

"Are you sure it was a good idea to bring Spark?" Amy asked Sam as the three cousins wheeled their bikes down the Chillinghurst station ramp and out on to the High Street.

The little dragon was tucked up in a new backpack. Sam's flat was huge, but Amy thought Aunt Jessica's new job must be keeping her very busy indeed for her not to have noticed a dragon moving in.

"Of course! She's going to help," Sam replied. "We came up with a great plan last night. It was going to be a surprise."

Charlie looked up at him from his phone. Amy knew he'd just texted his dad to let him know they'd arrived safely. "You and ... *she* ... made a plan?" he asked. "Together?"

"It was Spark's idea, really," Sam admitted. "Hey! I'm not crazy," he insisted. "She doesn't *speak* to me, but I kind of know what she's thinking."

Amy chewed her lip thoughtfully. Maybe there was a special link between Sam and the baby dragon? Weirder things had happened recently.

"Trust me," said Sam. "It'll be awesome!"

He leaned into his pedals. "You'll see!"

Amy and Charlie chased Sam down the street.

"This'll do!" he said suddenly, veering into a lane that sloped up under trees. They cycled after him up the steep incline.

They'd told their parents they wanted to get some proper exercise by cycling in the country for the day. *At least the exercise part was true*, Amy thought.

At the top of the hill, Sam dismounted and took Spark out of his backpack. The little dragon yawned and stretched her wings.

"Go for it, Spark!" cried Sam. Spark let out a series of musical squeaks then took to the air. "She's like our own private spy-drone," Sam said. "When she spots something freaky, she'll come back and tell us."

"That's brilliant!" Amy watched as Spark began flying in wide circles, spreading out further and further.

Suddenly, the dragon dived and vanished behind some trees.

They watched the skies for a while, then Amy gave an excited yell as Spark reappeared.

"She's found something," Sam exclaimed. "What is it, Spark?"

Spark let out a high-pitched cry and sped off along the track.

"Follow her!" yelled Sam, leaping on to his bike.

There was a bumpy chase until Spark came to rest on a set of wrought iron gates.

"Look at that!" Amy pointed at two circles of iron set in the gates. "Just like the symbols on our bracelets!"

Charlie stepped closer. "Except the design inside looks like slitted cat's eyes," he added.

"Like the ones I saw in the smoke yesterday," Sam said. "Great work, Spark – this has to be the right place!"

"But how do we get through?" Amy asked, grabbing the gates and rattling them. "They're locked tight."

"Watch out!" yelled Charlie.

Amy threw herself back. The slitted eyes were glowing red. A moment later, the red turned to silver, and with a *clank* and a *creak*, the gates opened.

"I guess that means we're allowed in," said Sam.

"This could be a trap," warned Charlie.

Spark leaped from the gates and flew down the path ahead, disappearing around a bend.

"You guys do what you like," said Sam, leaping on to his bike. "I'm going after her."

Amy didn't think twice before speeding after Sam. She heard Charlie right behind. After skimming around several bends, they came to a screeching halt. Ahead of them stood a breathtaking building of white stone.

Towers and spires rose above a high white wall pierced through by an ornate gateway with iron-studded doors and a half-raised portcullis. Arrow-slits stared blindly down at them; yellow and red banners flew from high rooftops.

"What *is* this?" gasped Amy. She couldn't decide whether it was a palace or a castle or both – but either way, it looked like it had come straight out of a folktale!

As she stared in astonishment, the building's heavy doors swung open.

"Someone definitely knows we're here,"

said Sam, laying down his bike. "Be ready for anything, guys!" Spark settled on his shoulder as he stepped through the doors.

They came into a wide hallway with a ceiling that soared up into shadows. As they walked across the marble floor, torches on both walls sprang into life.

"Well, this isn't creepy at all," whispered Charlie.

"It's kind of wonderful," breathed Amy.

They passed curved marble stairways, heading up to galleries and other floors. Banners hung from the walls, depicting some very odd creatures.

"This place is huge," Charlie mumbled.

They passed through several ornate

rooms, with doors that swung silently open for them and then closed behind with a *click*.

"Hey, lady!" Sam shouted. Amy nearly jumped out of her skin. Sam's voice echoed eerily in the silence. "Show yourself!"

"Why did you do that?" gasped Charlie.

"Because she obviously knows we're here and I'm bored of playing cat-and-mouse," Sam declared.

They walked through wide curved doors that opened before them.

"Awesome!" breathed Sam, his eyes like saucers.

Amy nodded her agreement as she turned a slow circle. It was a large, round room with a domed ceiling. The walls were covered in the most extraordinary murals Amy had ever seen – paintings showing fantastic landscapes filled with forests and waterfalls and snow-capped mountains; rivers that flowed through deep ravines, and foaming waves breaking against sea-gnawed cliffs.

The land was alive with huge and impossible creatures! Dragons and monstrous birds filled the skies; serpents and lizards lurked in the waters, mammoths and giant scorpions and a host of other nightmarish Beasts roamed the fields and hillsides.

There were people, as well. Men and

women dressed as warriors and wizards; queens and kings. At the heart of the vast mural, facing the doors, was a tall, broad-shouldered man, bearded and proud. The man held a shining sword up high, and a curious-looking shield hung on his left arm. Amy was drawn across the room by his piercing blue eyes. She stood directly under him, gazing up in awe.

Sam and Charlie stood on either side of Amy, as though they had also been pulled there by the man's eyes.

"It looks like something out of a fantasy movie," Charlie said softly.

"I'm not so sure," Amy replied. "I think these things are real ..." There was something about the strange creatures and the wonders of the stunning landscape that tugged at a place deep inside her. She felt it when she looked at the depictions of the man with the strange shield, too. The glint in his sharp blue eyes felt impossibly familiar.

"You're right," said Sam. "I think *this* is Avantia."

As he spoke the name, the doors slammed shut and a whirring noise sounded from above their heads.

Charlie ran for the doors. "We have to get out of here!" he yelled.

"No! Charlie, watch out!" Amy had seen the cause of the whirring. A great circular chandelier, ringed with sharp blades, dropped towards Charlie, spinning fast. Amy flung herself at Charlie, knocking him aside and landing on top of him.

The chandelier hit the floor and ground to a halt, spraying shards of glass. Sam threw himself down as splinters flew past him, embedding themselves in the wall.

Amy sprang up, helping the dazed Charlie to his feet.

"Someone is out to get us," said Sam, picking himself up.

"Someone, or some*thing*!" groaned Charlie, pointing a shaking finger at the wall. Amy turned and her heart leaped into her mouth. One of the creatures in the mural had come to terrifying life.

It was like a huge, mutated octopus with two joined heads and six cold, ice-blue eyes. As Amy watched in disgust, it crawled out of the painting, its bloated blue body blotched with green and yellow scabs, its inhuman eyes glaring with malice. Slithering tentacles reached towards them.

Charlie fell with a cry as a barbed tentacle wrapped around his ankle. With hideous strength, the creature dragged him towards its gaping maw.

SEVEN

Sam leaped forwards, his bracelet flowing out to form the now familiar chain and hook. He launched the weapon and it sank into the monster's tentacle. The octopus screeched as Sam leaned back, yanking on the hook.

Letting out a sudden shriek of fear, Spark sprang from Sam's shoulder.

Sam spun around and gazed upwards, his heart almost stopping. A fearsome bird hung in the air on vast, curved wings, a horrible stench wafting off its dark, oily feathers. The creature's bald head extended on a wizened neck, the beak gaping to reveal a deep red throat. Hooked claws reached out, spraying hot smoke as it snatched at Spark.

He heard a scream of rage at his back and glanced over his shoulder. Amy was standing astride the tentacle that held Charlie, hammering at it with her mace as blue blood spurted.

Sam released his hook and swung it up at the bird. But the creature's eyes blazed, and two red beams scythed down, knocking the hook away. He hurled himself aside as

the beams struck the ground, sending up spouts of smoke. He jumped up, his hook morphing into a round shield just in time to deflect two more deadly eye-beams.

From the corner of his eye, Sam saw tentacles swarming around Amy as the sharp spikes of her mace struck the limb that held Charlie.

Charlie sprang up, the battle-axe appearing in his hands. He began hacking at the tentacles as the octopus creature heaved and shrieked.

Everything was happening so fast, that there was hardly time to think. *I need the shield or I'm going to get fried by that bird's eyes*, Sam thought. *But that means I won't have the hook!*

"Tell Spark to blow smoke in its eyes!" Charlie yelled at Sam. The little dragon was flying around the monster's head, hissing and spitting.

"Spark!" Sam called. "Do your smoke thing!"

Spark sent out a burst of thick black smoke, which quickly enveloped the bird's head. It backed away, screaming, its wings cupping the air, sending down a stinking wind.

"Amy! Watch out!" shouted Sam as a barbed tentacle slithered around her waist, pinning her mace to her side and lifting her off the ground.

No, you don't!

Sam ran forward, his shield changing back to the hook and chain. He aimed the hook at the place where the octopus's two pulsating heads connected.

Thunnnkkk!

The beaked mouth stretched in a deafening scream. Tentacles thrashed as Sam threw his weight backwards and yanked on the chain, forcing the hook deeper into the creature's flesh.

Sam fell backwards as the hook came loose and Amy was flung through the air. A moment later, the octopus erupted into a cloud of blue ink that evaporated.

"Where did it go?" gasped Sam, stunned

to see that the monster had vanished.

"You killed it," panted Charlie. "One down ..."

"One to go!" Sam nodded, his heart pounding. "Where's Amy?" he asked. Last time he'd seen her, she had been flying across the room.

"Up here!" His eyes followed the sound up to where Amy was clinging to one of the giant bird's legs. As he watched, she struck upwards, her mace sinking into the matted black feathers on the monster's chest.

The bird arched upwards with a deafening screech – then exploded into a shower of black ink that faded away as it cascaded down.

Amy dropped, landing neatly on her feet.

Panting for breath, the three cousins came together in the middle of the room. Spark settled on Sam's shoulder, squeaking happily.

"That was so cool!" gasped Amy, wiping inky blood off her face with her sleeve.

"See how we worked together?" said Charlie excitedly. "We're a team!"

Sam stared at the painted walls. "Do you think there'll be more?"

"No way," said Amy. "They know better than to mess with us."

The doors slowly began to open.

"I think we've passed some kind of test," said Charlie. "Now we get to leave."

"Are you sure about that?" asked Sam, peering between the widening doors. In the darkness beyond, he saw a huge pair of slitted violet eyes.

Uh-oh! Seen them before!

There was a rumbling growl.

A large, powerful shape bounded into the room.

It was a panther, long and sleek and rippling with muscles, its fur the dark blue of the night sky before dawn. And it was the size of a horse!

It's really beautiful ... but super scary, too!

The panther bounded into the room, slamming into them, knocking Charlie and Amy aside. Its huge head struck Sam in the chest and he was sent crashing on to his back. Spark went bowling across the floor.

The panther's paw came down heavily on Sam's chest, pinning him down.

A huge head loomed above his face, the eyes shining.

The panther's jaws opened and Sam stared up at rows of razor-sharp fangs.

EIGHT

Charlie scrambled to his feet, dazed but ready with his battle-axe. The panther's jaws gaped above Sam's terrified face.

"That's enough, Varla!" a woman's voice rang out from the doorway.

She strode into the room, her purple-streaked hair streaming.

"Did *you* set those things on us?" Amy asked angrily.

"I had to test you," the woman said as

the panther loped to her side. "Simply wearing Arcane Bands does not make you Guardians. But you fought well."

"Those things could have killed us!" Charlie exclaimed.

"They are not true Beasts, but mere illusions," countered the woman. Then she bowed. "I am Karita of Banquise, Guardian of Avantia, bound by blood to the Sigil of Stealth. Now, I must know more about you." She pointed to Sam. "What is your name, and from where do you come?"

"We're not telling you anything till we know a whole lot more about *you*," Sam retorted. "And we've got weapons – so don't mess with us."

108

Varla growled, showing her teeth.

"I wish you no harm," Karita said. "But Varla will defend me to the death."

"Just tell her what she wants to know," said Charlie.

Sam glared at the woman. "I'm Sam Stonewin."

"Ah – a descendant of Dell of Stonewin?"

"Dell Stonewin was my grandfather," said Sam in surprise.

Karita turned to Amy. "And you, child?"

"Amy Errinel-Li."

Karita looked puzzled.

"My father is English," Amy explained, "and my mother is Chinese – they decided to use both names."

"Do you know the name Fern of Errinel?" asked Karita.

Amy nodded. "My grandmother. She died recently." She showed Karita her bracelet. "She left these for us. What did you call them?"

"Arcane Bands," said Karita. A hint of sadness came into her voice. "So, Fern of Errinel is no more," she sighed. "She must have been a great age."

"She was ninety-five," said Charlie. "And I'm Charlie Colton, before you ask. Are you going to tell me the name of *my* grandfather now?"

"Gustus of Colton," said Karita.

Wow! How does she know this stuff? "He

was my dad's dad," Charlie agreed. "Now it's your turn to answer some questions."

"Come," said Karita, turning and walking from the room with Varla pacing silently at her side. "Much shall be revealed."

She led them to a smaller chamber dominated by a huge mirror. She stood in front of it, taking a white crystal from a box and holding it up.

"Speak, Master of Beasts," she called.

The reflection in the mirror began to ripple.

Karita stepped aside as the figure of a man appeared in the mirror. A bearded man in full armour, his fist on the hilt of his sheathed sword, a strange-looking shield on his arm.

"That's the guy from the painting!" gasped Sam.

As he stared up into the man's clear blue eyes, Charlie somehow felt certain he could trust him.

"Greetings, Guardians of Avantia," said the man.

"Uhm ... hi," said Sam, but the man just kept on speaking.

It's some kind of hologram, Charlie realised.

"The Circle of Wizards has sent these message crystals to every realm known to them – on Avantia's own plane, and beyond," continued the man. "The portal through which you fell took you to a place beyond our understanding, but we will do everything in our power to find you, and bring you home again." His voice became graver: "You are in peril, Guardians. Malvel also passed through the portal – he is with you in that strange land." The blue eyes flashed. "This means a great burden has fallen on your shoulders. The Dark Wizard must not lay hands on the Beast eggs that he covets – you must protect them to your last breath. Stay strong, my friends ..." He drew his sword, and its blade gleamed like silver. "While there is blood in my veins, I will not stop looking for you!"

The image faded, leaving Charlie and

the others feeling stunned.

"So we're *Guardians*?" said Amy.

Karita nodded. "That is why my gates opened for you. Follow me." She took a side door and led them into a smaller room, where a table was laid with food and drink.

"The man who spoke was Tom, Avantia's legendary Master of the Beasts," she told them as she ushered them to seats. "A great hero."

"What did he mean by 'portal'?" asked Sam.

"It's a kind of doorway," Charlie said.

Amy frowned. "We never fell through a portal."

"Tom's message was for your ancestors,"

said Karita. "There was a great battle and Malvel, the Dark Wizard, created a portal to escape Tom and the Guardians. But the portal became unstable. Gustus, Fern and Dell went through first – Gustus carrying the chest with the eggs." She sighed. "But the portal's magic was breaking down, and when I followed Malvel, we arrived in this world at a different time, many years after my friends." She stroked Varla's head. "It appears fate decided that I should meet their grandchildren."

"How long have you been on Earth?" asked Charlie.

"Twenty years this summer," said Karita. "And if Fern of Errinel was ninety-five, then that means they came through eighty years ago." She shook her head sadly. "To think Fern and the others were so nearby, and I never found them. They must have concealed their magic well." She looked up at them. "Tell me how you came to hatch a dragon."

Sam fed Spark scraps from his plate as he and the others explained everything that had happened since the reading of Fern's will.

Karita nodded, asking occasional questions as they spoke.

"Why are these eggs so important?" Charlie asked her.

"Each egg holds a dormant Beast," Karita

117

told them. "Malvel wishes to hatch the eggs so that he can draw the power of the Beasts to himself and become invincible." She gave a grim smile. "I believe that Fern, Dell and Gustus hid the eggs in secret places all across this world."

"So Malvel couldn't get his hands on them," said Amy. "That's smart!"

"When I leaped into this realm, I had one egg with me," said Karita. "Although I knew it was perilous to unleash a Beast in this world, I hatched it – and so Varla was born."

"Why was it perilous?" asked Amy.

"Beasts come with great magic," Karita explained. "And magic does not belong on Earth. It could plunge this world into chaos."

Sam's eyes widened in alarm. "Spark is going to cause chaos?"

"No," Karita replied. "With correct training by her Guardian, she will be a force for Good, not Evil." She paused for a moment. "Only a Guardian can hatch a Beast egg," she continued, "which is a mercy – because if Malvel could hatch them himself, this world would already be lost!"

"Do you know where Malvel is now?" Charlie asked.

Karita nodded grimly. "He has gained much wealth and power, and with it he is searching the world for the missing eggs." She shuddered. "I fear him ... The power he could leech from even a single Beast would make him a deadly threat."

Cold fingers crawled up Charlie's spine. "When we met you in the park yesterday, you said you *sensed* that Spark had hatched," he said. "Does that mean Malvel will have sensed it as well?"

Karita nodded again.

Charlie looked at his cousins. "You know what that means, don't you?" he gulped. "The Dark Wizard is coming for us!"

NINE

Amy knew her cousins were thinking the same thing she was: if Karita was frightened of Malvel, what chance did *they* stand?

"What if we decide we'd rather *not* be Guardians?" Charlie asked.

Karita frowned at him. "You all have the breath of heroes in your lungs!" she said solemnly. "You and Sam vanquished Voltrex, the Two-headed Octopus." Her

121

gaze turned to Amy. "And you defeated Kronus the Clawed Menace. You are the descendants of Guardians and you each wear an Arcane Band."

"But how are we going to beat Malvel?" Charlie asked.

"We need to plan carefully. Choose our moment, strategise an attack, and then defeat him in mortal combat!" declared Karita.

Amy gulped. "And if we do defeat him?" she asked. "What then?"

"We will gather the Beast eggs and return home." Karita's eyes glazed over with emotion. "Avantia!" she breathed. "How I've longed for it!"

"But we're *already* home," Sam pointed out.

Karita arched an eyebrow at him. "Are you certain?" she asked. "Perhaps we must each decide for ourselves where we belong – but surely you all agree that this is no world for Beasts and magic?"

"So, you'd want to take Spark back to Avantia?" asked Sam.

"Yes, she must return to her own realm," said Karita.

Sam lowered his head, stroking Spark's wings as he stared at the table.

Charlie winced. *Poor Sam. He already loves that little dragon.*

"Come," said Karita, standing up. "Let

me show you some of the marvels of your homeland!"

She led them back to the mural room, gesturing to the painted landscape. "See, here is King Hugo's palace in the City, heart of the kingdom. And beyond it the Grassy Plains and the Northern Mountains."

Amy followed the line of Karita's pointing finger.

"And here is the mountain where Ferno the Fire Dragon lives." Karita sighed. "A Good Beast, and a loyal defender of Avantia."

"So, Beasts are Good?" asked Charlie.

"Some are ... but others are created for Evil," Karita replied. She pointed to a

ragged coastline lapped with blue waves. "The Western Ocean – home of Sepron, master of the tides."

"Good?" asked Amy.

"Good," agreed Karita, her finger moving on. "The Ruby Desert, Spindrel and the Winding River." She pointed to a village among trees. "Errinel, home of your ancestors, Amy. Do these names not waken memories?"

"Not really, "Amy admitted.

But *something* was stirring in her heart. Her grandmother and Charlie and Sam's grandfathers had kept the secret of their origins for all those years! And now the secret – and the responsibility that went with it – had been passed on to them. Their three families weren't connected by blood, but maybe they were bound together by something just as powerful.

It was frightening, but it was also wonderful.

Tears glistened in Karita's eyes. "Together, we may be able to defeat Malvel, and form a portal to Avantia."

It must have been awful, being alone all this time, Amy thought. *No wonder Karita wants to go home.*

Charlie looked at his Arcane Band. "How do these things work?" he asked.

"They know your needs and act accordingly," Karita explained. "A shield for defence, a weapon for attack. But Arcane Bands do not make Guardians – you will need training to unleash all your Avantian abilities."

"Can *you* train us?" asked Amy.

"I can," said Karita, smiling. "Just as Tom once trained me and your grandparents. You give me new heart! Follow me – let the training commence!"

Amy grinned at Charlie as Karita led them out of the mural room. "Are you up for this?" she asked.

Charlie looked uneasy. "I'm not as sporty as you and Sam," he admitted. "I'm worried I'll let you down."

"You won't," Amy said. "You'll do just

fine – won't he, Sam?" She looked around. "Sam?"

But there was no sign of their cousin ... or his baby dragon.

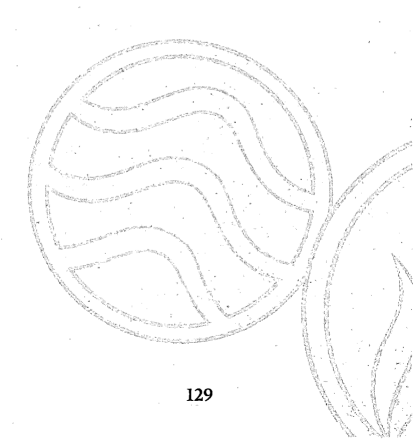

TEN

Sam powered down Chillinghurst High Street, travelling at top speed. His feet dug at the pedals, his thigh muscles aching. He leaned over the handlebars, cycling with all his might. Spark sat on his shoulder, trilling happily, her tail wrapped around his neck.

The phone in his pocket was buzzing. It was probably Charlie or Amy, texting him. They'd have noticed by now that he'd left.

Sorry, guys – it was great hanging out with you, and I get the whole destiny thing, but there's no way that lady is taking Spark!

He turned into the road that led to the railway station. His plan was to jump on the first train, no matter where it was going.

The station was ahead of him now. He sped past parked cars.

He could hear a train being announced.

Perfect timing! Hey! What on …

A sleek black saloon suddenly pulled out right in front of him.

Sam yanked on the brakes and came skidding to a halt, his heart pumping at the near miss. He glared at the windscreen.

"Watch it, mister!" he shouted.

The driver stared at him through black sunglasses. He was a big guy – like a tank in a suit – and had a face like a slab of stone.

A back window rolled down.

"Sam Stonewin? Is that you?"

Sam walked his bike around to the side of the car.

"Oh – hi, Mr Haynecroft," Sam said in surprise. He'd met his mother's boss once, but he mostly recognised him from internet articles. "Your driver nearly ran me over."

What on earth is he doing here?

Sam was aware of movement along his spine as Spark dived into his backpack.

"My sincere apologies for startling you,

Sam," said Mr Haynecroft, opening the car's door. "Come inside while you recover from the shock."

Sam peered into the plush interior of the car.

"I need to catch this train," he said.

"Nonsense," said Mr Haynecroft, opening the door wider. "I insist!"

Sam felt a twinge of unease. He turned his bike away from the car. "Places to be, people to see," he said lightly. "Nice to see you, sir."

"Obey me!" Mr Haynecroft's voice took on a hard edge. "Get into the car!"

Whoa! Who does this guy think he is? I need to get out of here.

"Not going to happen," said Sam, but before he could move, the driver's door sprang open and Tank Man stepped into his path.

Uh-oh!

Sam lifted the bike and turned it around, jumping into the saddle and speeding down the road. Glancing over his shoulder, he saw that Tank Man was back at the wheel – the car was coming for him.

I need to get off the road unless I want to become a decoration on that bumper!

He turned into the high road and whizzed along, looking for a narrow lane or side street where the car couldn't go.

There!

An alley led between two buildings – wide enough for his bike's handlebars, but not for Mr Haynecroft's car.

"See ya, suckers!" Sam called back as he dived into the alley, exhilarated at his escape – even if he still didn't know exactly *what* he was escaping.

The path wound upwards through thick trees, getting steeper as he left the village behind. He began to struggle with the slope. The trees crowded in on all sides.

What now?

I know! Send Spark for help!

He halted and opened his backpack. "Spark – come on out. I need you to find Charlie and Amy. Tell them I need their help."

The little dragon sprang out of the backpack and took to the air, just as a sudden, fierce wind lashed Sam in the face. The trees shook, the branches thrashing so that leaves were ripped off.

Sam gaped in astonishment as the flying leaves began to whirl in front of him like a hurricane.

A figure appeared within the whirlwind. It lifted its arms and the leaves exploded in all directions.

Sam stared in absolute disbelief.

"Mr Haynecroft?" he gasped.

Mr Haynecroft flicked a few leaf-shreds off his suit then turned his dark eyes on Sam. "You cannot outrun me, boy."

Sam tried to turn his bike around.

Mr Haynecroft lifted his hand and a ball of green fire erupted from his palm. Sam only just managed to throw himself clear as the green fire blasted the bike.

It crashed against a tree, a scorched, twisted wreck.

"Who are you?" Sam gasped, his blood racing, his heart beating hard against his ribs.

"I am *power!*" said Mr Haynecroft, raising his arms. Sam watched in terror as the man's clothing changed – where there had been a smart business suit, now he was clad in dark green robes, and a great black cloak hung from his arms like bat wings.

The man's voice boomed in Sam's ears, driving him to his knees.

"I am the Dark Wizard!" he roared. "My name is Malvel!"

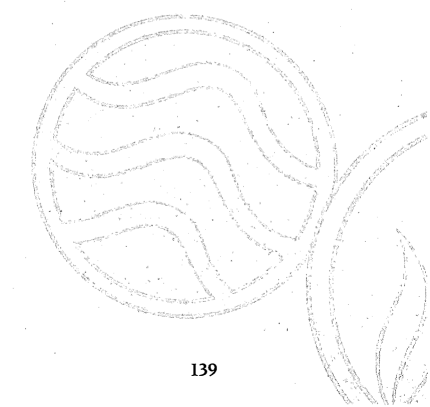

ELEVEN

"**D**on't lose her!" Charlie cried as Karita turned her speeding four-wheel drive on to Chillinghurst High Street.

"There!" gasped Amy, pointing ahead.

The little dragon cut through the air as they sped after her.

It had all happened very quickly.

They had just started discussing what to do about Sam's disappearance when Spark had come crashing through a window, screeching in panic.

It was obvious Sam was in trouble.

"Lead us to him!" Karita had said.

They had all piled into her car and the chase had begun.

At first, Varla had loped along beside the vehicle, her dark outline slipping in and out of the trees like a ghost. But now they were in the village, she leaped gracefully from rooftop to rooftop, easily keeping pace with them.

"How does she do that?" breathed Charlie.

"She's a Shadow Panther," said Karita. "A Beast of Stealth."

"Where's Spark?" gasped Amy.

Karita stepped on the brakes and the car came to a halt beside a narrow alleyway. "That way." She pointed between two buildings. "We must follow on foot."

They jumped out and raced into the alley. Charlie saw the little dragon zip into tall trees.

The alley led to a steep, climbing pathway through dense woodland. Karita led them up the hill. Charlie nearly jumped out of his skin as Varla bounded past him, silent as the wind, her long legs eating up the ground as she caught up with Karita.

He heard an ear-piercing screech from a little way ahead.

Spark hung in the air, screaming at the

top of her voice.

"Hush, child!" crooned Karita, holding up her arm. The dragon landed on her wrist, whimpering as she stared at the ground.

"That's Sam's bike," breathed Amy.

Charlie stared in horror at the twisted and tangled wreck. It lay crumpled beside a tree, smoking as though it had been hit by a missile.

What on earth did that?

"Is Sam close by?" Karita asked the panther. Varla sniffed the bike then lifted her head, her whiskers twitching as she tested the air.

She gave a soft growl. Charlie's stomach

dropped when he saw Karita's expression.

Varla can't smell Sam – that's not good!

"The stench of dark magic hangs heavy in this place," Karita said, her voice disgusted. "We came too late. Malvel has taken him."

"Taken him where?" Amy cried.

Karita drew out a tablet from her pocket. "To his lair, no doubt. I'll show you," she said, activating the tablet and tapping to access a file.

She held it up for the cousins to see. "This is the heart of the Dark Wizard's domain," she said. "None can pass its gates and live."

Charlie and Amy stared at a photo on the screen of a huge black office block, looming over a city skyline.

"But that's Obsidian Tower," exclaimed Amy.

"Malvel lives in Obsidian Tower?" said Charlie. "That's crazy ... unless ..." A terrible thought struck him. Karita had told them that Malvel had made himself rich and powerful. *Could it be ... ?*

"Why is Mr Haynecroft helping Malvel?" breathed Amy.

Charlie shook his head. "It's worse than that," he said. "Mr Haynecroft *is* Malvel!"

"Yes, Haynecroft is the name he uses in this realm," Karita told them. "As Alistair Haynecroft, Malvel has built a corporate empire that spans the world."

"And he's using Obsidian's resources to

look for the other eggs," said Charlie.

"We have to get in there and stop him!" Amy said determinedly.

Karita shook her head and touched the screen and a schematic of the tower appeared. She pointed to the top. "Sam will have been taken to Malvel's private offices on the one hundred and twentieth floor," she said. "His tower has some of the world's most advanced security systems. Sam is beyond our help now."

TWELVE

"Almost there," said Charlie as he tapped ferociously at his mobile phone.

"Great job!" Amy told her cousin. Charlie was a whiz with computers, but she was still amazed that he'd been able to access Obsidian's central network, beginning with nothing more what he'd guessed to be Aunt Jessica's logon ID.

They'd talked about going directly to Aunt Jessica for help in getting into

Obsidian Tower, but if she heard Sam was in danger Amy was sure Aunt Jessica would have wanted to confront her evil boss. But Haynecroft was the Dark Wizard himself – Amy hardly knew what to expect, but at least she and Charlie had their Arcane Bands to protect them. Aunt Jessica wouldn't have a chance, and Amy was certain Sam wouldn't want his mother in danger.

"OK, you ready?" asked Charlie.

"Ready!"

Charlie tapped the screen.

Amy looked at him. "Is that it? Did it work?"

"Give it a couple of—" The raucous

blaring of fire alarms cut off his words. Charlie grinned. "Piece of cake!"

"You are the most genius computer nerd ever!" breathed Amy.

"Thanks ... I think!"

Amy and Charlie were huddled behind a large wheelie bin in a service area behind Obsidian Tower.

They watched as the doors opened, and a few people trickled out. Most of them wore some kind of uniform – canteen staff and building maintenance workers, Amy assumed. The majority of the office workers would use the front entrances to evacuate. Although – since it was mid-evening on a Saturday – they were hoping that the building would be mostly empty.

Once the people had gone around the corner, towards the front of the building, Amy and Charlie slipped in quietly through the back doors. Charlie used the schematic of the building he'd called up on his phone to guide them to the lifts. Along the way, he used his access to the tower's security system to turn off cameras, motion sensors and security measures before they reached them.

With the building evacuated, they had the high-speed lift to themselves.

Amy watched the floors flick away on the digital display. She saw the tense look on her cousin's face. "We have Arcane Bands," she reminded him. "And the Dark Wizard doesn't."

"I'm worried about what he *does* have," muttered Charlie.

"Are you scared?" she asked.

"A bit," he admitted. "Aren't you?"

Do not let him see how terrified you are!

"Nope," she replied. "We're going to be awesome!"

The lift halted and the door slid open. The fire alarm had stopped.

Amy adjusted her processors as they stepped into a glass-walled corridor that ran alongside a row of high-tech laboratories. The place seemed deserted but lights flashed and blinked on electronic devices

151

and the air throbbed with a constant humming.

Charlie came to a stop and peered through a glass wall. "Whoa, that's got to be one of the Beast eggs," he said, pointing.

On a chrome bench, a large, colourful egg stood upright in a metal cradle while the articulated arms of complicated machines probed and drilled and shot lasers at it.

Malvel is trying to get it open.

Even as Amy stared through the glass, she saw a drill-bit snap off against the shell of the egg. The arm of the machine pulled back. The egg was unharmed.

"He's using science and technology,"

Charlie said. "That must mean his magic doesn't work on them." He glanced at Amy. "That's a good sign, right?"

But Amy heard something – something huge – coming for them. She turned to see a large man stumping towards them from the end of the corridor.

"That's *not* good," she murmured, her heart thumping.

"Uh-oh!" gulped Charlie, looking the other way.

There were two of them – huge men in black suits, their muscles straining at the cloth as they closed in from either side. Both were wearing sunglasses, and had square grey faces with wide, lipless mouths and heavy brows.

Amy pulled back her sleeve to reveal her Arcane Band. "Don't take another step!" she warned.

The men were only a couple of metres away now. Apart from the thud of their feet on the floor, they were completely silent.

"You asked for it!" Amy yelled. Her Band came alive, shooting out from her wrist to form the silver mace. Charlie's axe was in his hands a moment later.

One of the men reached out a huge hand for Amy. She ducked under his arm and brought the mace's head down hard on his fingers.

Gloiiinnnggg!

The mace rang off the man's hand, and pain shot up Amy's arm.

What is he made of – solid stone?

One of them punched at her head and she only just darted aside in time. His fist crashed through the glass wall behind her and the air filled with splintered shards.

She struck at the man's chest. The mace rang and turned aside, ripping through the fabric of his suit. Amy stared at a body formed of rough granite. She staggered back, colliding with Charlie.

They're not human! How do you fight living stone?

Charlie's axe had changed into a shield and the other monster's fists were pummelling it mercilessly, driving him back further and further.

Terrified, Amy jabbed up into the first monster's face. The sunglasses snapped off to reveal deep pits that glowed with a poisonous green light.

She heard Charlie give a cry. The other monster had caught hold of his shield and jerked him into the air, shaking him like a rag doll.

Then suddenly, the shield was gone and the axe was back in Charlie's grip. As he fell from between the creature's arms, he brought his axe down on its skull.

"Yow!" he cried out in pain as the axe twisted on the stone head – but the blow dislodged the sunglasses and Amy saw the monster's eye-pits, burning with a grisly yellow fire.

"This way!" Amy cried, diving headfirst through the shattered glass wall into the laboratory. Charlie flung himself after her and they scrambled around to the far side of the metal bench.

They heard the ponderous tread of the two stone men. Then there was silence.

"Pitiful!" sneered a cruel voice. "I had expected more from would-be Guardians."

Amy and Charlie lifted their eyes above the bench. Mr Haynecroft stood between the immobile monsters, but instead of a business suit, he wore dark green robes.

"Malvel!" spat Amy.

"I see you know my true name," Malvel said smoothly. "Was this feeble attack the Stealth Guardian's idea?"

"No!" shouted Charlie. "She told us not to – but we came anyway!"

"Give us back our cousin," Amy added.

"Fools! I *wanted* you to come here." Malvel laughed harshly. "You will hatch the Beast egg I found and I will absorb its power and be invincible!" His voice rose. "Let us bring this to an end ... Grom, Morg – speak!"

As Amy stared in horror, the two stone men opened their mouths and let out ear-piercing shrieks.

159

Charlie curled up on the floor, his hands crammed over his ears, his face wracked with pain.

Amy quickly slipped her magnetic headpieces off and an absolute silence descended. She got to her feet and lifted the egg out of its cradle. *Saving Beast eggs is what Guardians do!*

But before she could make another move, Malvel casually waved his hand in the air.

The egg jumped out of Amy's arms.

"Wait – *what*?" The egg glided across the room and dropped lightly to the ground. Amy saw that Malvel's two creatures had shut their mouths, so she scrambled to replace her headpieces so she could hear again.

"Who do you think you are dealing with, child?" Malvel asked. "I used the boy to lure you here. There is no escape. Do you think my minions have only one power?" He lifted his hands. "They contain the forces of the elements ... Obey me, and help me hatch this egg or I will unleash destruction that you cannot imagine! Or will you continue to waste my time?"

"I wouldn't say we're *wasting* time," Amy said, helping a very groggy-looking Charlie to his feet. "More like stalling, I'd say. What time is it, anyway, Charlie?"

Charlie took out his phone out. The

screen displayed a countdown.

$$00{:}02$$

$$00{:}01$$

$$00{:}00$$

"It's showtime!" he said with a smile.

At that exact moment, the windows behind them exploded inwards and Varla burst into the room with Karita mounted on her back. Spark was with them, breathing red fire.

"Looks like you're the one who doesn't know who they're dealing with!" yelled Amy, raising her mace as she ran at the Dark Wizard.

THIRTEEN

Sam sat on the floor in a store room, chained to a steel shelving unit. A little while ago, a fire alarm had sounded, but it was gone now.

What's happening out there?

A shrieking noise shook the air for a few moments, and the image of the little dragon filled his mind.

"Spark!"

He got to his feet, staring at the door.

Waiting.

The door burst open and Spark flew in, breathing red flame.

"Way to go!" Sam yelled. "And you can breathe fire now! Cool!"

The dragon chirruped in delight.

"A little help?" Sam said, holding up his chained arm. Spark landed on his shoulder and spat a jet of flame that melted the chain.

He ran from the cupboard into a laboratory of some kind. He found his Arcane Band on an examination table and quickly slipped it on to his wrist. There was wail of piercing noise from somewhere nearby. As he raced around the corner with Spark flying over his head, his Band changed into the hook and chain.

Something was going on in a huge laboratory space with a smashed glass wall. Green light flashed on and off, crisscrossing the room like emerald lightning, exploding off the walls, ricocheting off the floor and ceiling. The magical green fire was coming from Malvel's hands as he tried to strike Karita and Varla. But Karita and her Stealth Panther kept vanishing and reappearing behind him so that Malvel had to twist and turn to defend himself. Sam saw fury in the Dark Wizard's face.

Boy – is he mad!

But that wasn't all. Charlie and Amy were

battling with two of Malvel's huge stone men – and they weren't doing brilliantly. They were crouching in a corner under silver shields while the monsters rained blows down on them with fists like piledrivers.

"Let's go, Spark!" said Sam.

Spark flew at one of the men, scorching his back with a blast of flame. The creature's clothes caught fire and he thrashed about as Spark enveloped him in a cloud of thick black smoke.

Sam swung his chain and released. The hook caught around the second creature's neck, sending splinters of rock shooting around the room. Sam jerked back as the stone man clutched at his throat.

This is too easy!

The monster turned and Sam stared in alarm at two burning yellow pits where the eyes should have been.

Uh-oh! These things aren't even close *to human!*

A blast of sulphurous fire exploded from the stone man's eyes. Sam threw himself to the floor as the fire gushed above him, scorching his clothing and striking the far wall. He scrambled across the floor as the creature turned his head, his eyes gushing flame.

Charlie and Amy were back on their feet, hacking at one of the creatures with mace and axe. The monster's clothing was in tatters, but his granite skin fended off every blow.

Sam reeled in his hook and flung it again, aiming low. The chain wrapped around one thick ankle. He scrambled behind a steel workbench, jamming his feet against it as he hauled back with all his might.

The stone man staggered and fell, the yellow fire spraying up on to the ceiling in a deadly fountain.

He's down ... Now what?

Charlie's axe changed into a shield as he sprang forwards. He brought the shield down on to the creature, bouncing the searing flames back into its face.

He's using the guy's own power against him. That's genius!

Amy flung herself at the shield to help Charlie overpower the stone man's sinister energies. Sam saw the trapped fires seething underneath them.

He bounded across the room, landing on top of Charlie to help his cousins hold the shield in place.

There was an explosion beneath them and they collapsed in a heap as the stone man's head shattered into fragments – a victim of his own fire.

They helped each other up, breathless but victorious.

The second stone man was staggering

blindly about the lab, crashing into benches and cabinets while Spark circled his head, spitting flame and smoke.

"Go, team!" Sam yelled. He turned to his cousins. "Amy – watch out!"

The deadly battle of tag between Malvel and Karita and Varla had come very close. The Dark Wizard grabbed Amy around the waist, pulling her backwards as he tried to rip the Arcane Band from her arm. Her mace swept through the air, but she couldn't hit him.

Karita appeared in front of them. "Amy, duck!" She cracked the bo-staff against Malvel's shoulder, sending him reeling. His arm was still around Amy's middle and she was dragged with him, doubling over with a cry as they struck the wall.

Something slipped from Amy's shirtfront and hung loose.

It was the amulet they'd found in Fern's cellar.

Malvel's eyes blazed.

"The Seeing Eye!" he shouted, ripping the amulet from Amy's neck and flinging her aside. "At last, it's mine!"

Laughing wildly, he held the amulet up. He pointed a finger at it and green fire splashed over the ruby stone.

A cone of white light poured from the amulet and projected a series of pictures before them. *A woman's face carved in gold.*

A large clock face against a field of green. A spiny, serpent-like creature twisted into a ring.

Sam gasped in awe. The images fired one after another. *A row of columns in the desert. A wall made of grinning skulls.*

"Clues to the location of every Beast egg in this world!" crowed Malvel. Sam saw that Malvel was as mesmerised by the images as he was.

The Stealth Panther decided to take advantage of Malvel's distraction. She pounced, her midnight-blue body arcing across the room, her jaws wide and her claws unsheathed.

"No, Varla!" shouted Karita.

But it was too late. Looping the amulet around his neck, Malvel aimed a blast of green fire at the panther, who fell with a cry. Malvel loomed over her, twisting the emerald gem of a ring on his forefinger.

"Give me your power, Beast of Avantia!" he cried as the gem flared, bathing Varla in a sickly light.

Sam watched in horror as the panther shrank, her rich blue coat dulling to grey, the magical light fading from her eyes.

Amy screamed, her hands over her face.

"We have to stop him!" Sam yelled, running forward.

Amy's mace flashed, and Charlie was on his feet again, gripping his axe.

Varla was mewling pitifully, her body shrunk to the size of an ordinary pet cat.

A scream made Sam look back in alarm.

"*Varla!*" Karita stared at the withered panther in horror then reeled and collapsed.

Malvel's laughter swelled as he got to his feet.

"Finally, I have the power of a Beast!" he roared, spreading his arms, his hands blazing green. "Now you will never be able to stop me!"

FOURTEEN

Charlie raced to help Karita. She was crawling weakly across the floor, reaching out for her injured Beast.

"Save yourselves," she groaned. "All my powers are gone!"

A poison-green flare lit up the laboratory, a wave of power that knocked Charlie off his feet.

He blinked to clear the dazzle from his eyes. The spell had been aimed at Spark and the little dragon had tumbled through the window. The remaining stone man was clear of smoke now. He was attacking Amy, who dodged his furious blows, parrying them with swings of her mace to protect her head and implants. She leaped high to avoid the flames that shot from the stone man's eyes.

How long can she hold him off?

Sam was running to help her, but was knocked down by a magic blast striking his shoulder. Malvel's hands glowed with blinding green light and there was a horrible glee in his expression.

He's enjoying hurting us!

Anger welled in Charlie and he ran at the

sorcerer, his axe clutched in both hands.

Malvel sent him flying with a flick of his fingers. Pain ripped through Charlie's chest, but he set his jaw and got to his feet again. This time, he managed to deflect the wizard's blast with the blade of his axe.

He had given Sam the chance to get to his feet and swing his grappling hook.

Sam released and the hook spun out, its long chain winding around Malvel's chest.

"Gotcha!" Sam yelled, pulling back.

Malvel let out a cry of rage as Sam jerked him off-balance.

For a moment, it seemed as though Malvel might fall – but then he wrapped the chain around one arm and hauled on it.

Caught unawares, Sam tottered forwards into twin blasts from the stone man's eyes.

Charlie was horrified to see Sam engulfed in fire. The hook and chain melted away.

"No!" cried Charlie as Malvel sent out another burst of flame that threw Sam across the room.

He'll kill him!

But maybe there was still a chance to save Sam ...

Charlie bounded across the room and jumped on to the bench where electronic instruments had been probing the egg.

He twisted the laser arm around, aiming it at Malvel. He scanned the control panel, quickly grasping how it worked.

He slammed his hand down on the power button.

A thin beam of white light shot across the room, striking Malvel in the chest. The Dark Wizard reeled back, his face seething with rage.

"You would dare ... ?" he howled.

"You bet I would!" shouted Charlie, twisting a dial to increase the power of the laser beam.

"Grom! Protect your master!" roared the wizard. The stone man lurched between Malvel and the laser beam.

Amy ran to where Sam lay huddled against the wall. Charlie twisted the dial to maximum. He turned just in time to see the remaining stone man lift Malvel into his arms before crashing through the laboratory wall and out of sight.

Charlie leaped off the bench and ran to where Amy was crouching at Sam's side.

He skidded to a halt. Sam was sitting up, looking a little dazed, but otherwise OK.

"Why aren't you burned to a crisp?" Charlie cried.

"It wasn't that hot," said Sam.

"Sam! You're *still* on fire!" gasped Amy, pointing at the flames licking along Sam's sleeve.

"Whoa, yeah, I am!" Sam patted at the flames and they died away. He looked at Charlie and Amy. "What?" he asked as they stared at him.

"You should be medium rare at the very least!" Charlie said in disbelief.

Just then Spark swooped back in through the window. She settled happily on Sam's shoulder, nuzzling at his head.

"His bond with the dragon protects him from fire," said a voice behind them.

Charlie looked around. His heart clenched when he saw Karita, holding the limp form of Varla in her arms.

The poor thing – she's so badly hurt!

"The bond between a Beast and the Guardian who hatches it is deep and strong," Karita said, kissing the shrunken panther's head. "It changes both for ever."

She looked at Sam. "Forgive me, I should never have suggested taking Spark from you. I know that's why you ran from the castle. This is all my fault."

"No, it's Malvel's fault!" snarled Charlie. "We'll make him pay for what he's done!"

Amy got to her feet. "Where did he go?"

Charlie pointed to the hole in the wall. "The second stone man took him," he said.

"They can't have got far," exclaimed Sam, jumping up. "I'm the fireproof one – you guys keep behind me!"

Karita laid Varla lovingly on the floor, briefly stroking her head as she mewed weakly. There was a ferocious light in her eyes as she straightened up, the bo-staff suddenly in her hand. Charlie caught a glint beneath her sleeve.

The staff comes from her Arcane Band! I never realised that.

"Malvel!" Karita shouted, raising the bo-staff into the air. "Hear me! While there is breath in my lungs I will fight you!"

"What's that noise?" asked Sam.

"It's coming from the roof!" Amy said.

Sam ran to the broken window. "A helicopter!" He flung out his arm and the hook and chain spun into the night.

Charlie raced to the window. The helicopter was flying away from the building, gathering speed.

Sam's hook fell short and with a cry of

frustration he reeled it back in.

"He's getting away!" said Amy.

"Malvel has the Seeing Eye," said Karita. "With the clues within, he will be able to gather all the Beast eggs." Her head drooped. "I have failed."

"No, you haven't," said Sam. "We'll find him and we'll stop him."

Karita looked at him, her eyes full of doubt.

"Thanks to you, we know who we are now," Amy added. "We're a team – just as Gran and the others would have wanted."

"Plus we have our own fire-breathing dragon," said Charlie, looking at Karita. "Amy saved the Beast egg Malvel was experimenting on, and besides ..." He held up his phone. "We have the clues, too."

"You mean—" Amy gaped at him.

"You filmed those magical holograms?" Sam said. He looked as stunned as Amy.

"Well, they seemed pretty important," Charlie said. "Right? *Oof* ..." Amy and Sam both simultaneously hugged their cousin.

"So: a Beast egg, a dragon and a phone full of clues," said Amy, turning to Karita, "That's a good start, isn't it?"

Karita smiled faintly. "It is," she conceded. "It is a very good start."

Charlie grinned at her. "And like you said – we've got the breath of heroes in our lungs."

"And while there's breath in our lungs, we'll keep fighting," added Amy, as the three cousins looked at each other. "Because that's what Guardians do!"

THE END

BeastQuest

NEW BLOOD

A D A M B L A D E

Amy, Sam and Charlie's
adventures continue in

New Blood 2:
The Dark Wizard

Turn the page for a sneak peek ...

Malvel's eyes gleamed. "Now we will roam the world, hunting down the Beast eggs one by one, until I have them all in my grasp."

"And then ... ?" breathed Illia Raven, head of Research and Development at Obsidian. "Will you capture one of the child Guardians and have them hatch the eggs for you?" Malvel had told her that only Guardians had the ability to hatch Avantian Beast eggs.

Malvel was silent for a few moments. "I took the power of the Shadow Panther," he said at last. "It flows through my veins." Illia bit her lip as she saw the sinister purple light burn more fiercely in the Dark Wizard's eyes. "I might now be able to hatch the eggs myself," the wizard continued, "absorbing their power, becoming stronger and stronger!"

"And when you have all that power," said Illia, "will you return to Avantia?"

Illia was human, but she knew that portals could be opened between realms, and she knew that Malvel's ultimate intention was to return to his home world and become the Tyrant of Avantia.

"When the Earth is mine and its people kneel before me, I will go back and fulfil my destiny!"

"When you leave Earth, you will need a trusted lieutenant to rule in your place," Illia said.

Malvel looked narrowly at her. "Would you like that to be you?"

"I would!" Illia exclaimed. "I will rule this planet in your name, and anyone who defies me will be crushed."

A faint smile curled Malvel's lip. "Grand words, Illia," he said. "But I will need proof that you are worthy."

Illia stiffened, her eyes blazing. "Try me!"

"Very well," said the Wizard. "I will give you a mission to test your abilities – and to get those Guardian children out of the way ... *for ever.*"

Illia Raven leaned forward eagerly. If the three children had to die to prove her worth, then Amy Errinel-Li, Charlie Colton and Sam Stonewin were doomed.

Look out for
New Blood 2: The Dark Wizard
to find out what happens next!